THIS BOOK BELONGS TO

....

Copyright © 2015

make believe ideas ltd

The Wilderness, Berkhamsted, Hertfordshire, HP4 2AZ, UK.

www.makebelieveideas.com

CINDERELLA

Written by Helen Anderton
Illustrated by Stuart Lynch

make
believe
ideas

Reading together

This book is designed to be fun for children who are gaining confidence in their reading. They will enjoy and benefit from some time discussing the story with an adult. Here are some ways you can help your child take those first steps in reading:

❄ Encourage your child to look at the pictures and talk about what is happening in the story.

❄ Help your child to find familiar words and sound out the letters in harder words.

❄ Ask your child to read and repeat each short sentence.

Look at rhymes

Many of the sentences in this book are simple rhymes. Encourage your child to recognise rhyming words. Try asking the following questions:

❄ What does this word say?

❄ Can you find a word that rhymes with it?

❄ Look at the ending of two words that rhyme. Are they spelt the same? For example, "chance" and "dance", and "soap" and "rope".

Reading activities

The **What happens next?** activity encourages your child to retell the story and point to the mixed-up pictures in the right order.

The **Rhyming words** activity takes six words from the story and asks your child to read and find other words that rhyme with them.

The **Key words** pages provide practice with common words used in the context of the book. Read the sentences with your child and encourage him or her to make up more sentences using the key words listed around the border.

A **Picture dictionary** page asks children to focus closely on nine words from the story. Encourage your child to look carefully at each word, cover it with his or her hand, write it on a separate piece of paper, and finally, check it!

Do not complete all the activities at once – doing one each time you read will ensure that your child continues to enjoy the story and the time you are spending together. Have fun!

Once, a girl called Cinderella
was locked up in a gloomy cellar
by Eve and Val, her jealous sisters
(next to her, they looked like blisters).

6

Then one day, an invitation
    was sent to each home in the nation.
"Prince Billy is looking to be wed.
    Come to the royal ball!" it said.

Invitation

7

"Huzzah!" yelled Cinders, "Just the fella
   to free me from this gloomy cellar!"
Eve and Val declared, "Fat chance!
   YOU'RE not going to the dance!"

They locked her up with ghastly grins,
   and powdered both their slimy chins.
Then they left and Cinders wept,
   but luckily, just then in stepped . . .

a courgette fairy, full of cheer!
        She said, "I'm here to help, my dear.
I'll get you to the ball tonight,
        with courgette tools of green and white!"

She brought one out, quite long and green:
    it turned into a limousine!
Soon, Cinders had a brand-new dress
    and two shoes — made of glass, no less!

"At midnight," said the fairy, "flee,
or a courgette you will be!"
So Cinders left in her new ride,
with bright green, soggy seats inside!

In no time, she was at the palace.

The prince looked lonely and embarrassed.

He scowled, "I'm hungry! I won't dance!

Have you got snacks, by any chance?"

Cinders knew just what to do.

She said, "I have a treat for you!

Try my courgette limousine:

the bright green, scrumptious, car canteen!"

14

After their snack of courgette car,
    the pair felt happier by far
and so began to dance around,
    while Eve and Val just watched and frowned.

But soon, the clock began to strike –
    there was no time to say goodnight!
Cinders ran, but in her haste,
    she left one shoe at Billy's place!

Billy vowed, "I'll search for you –
the girl who fits this tiny shoe!"
But though the prince went far and wide,
no girl could get her foot inside!

Some tried tape and some tried glue.
	Some got angry at the shoe.
Some greased up their feet with soap –
	one even tied her toes with rope!

Soon, Billy got to Cinders' door,
    but she was locked downstairs once more.
Eve and Val were there instead.
    "Try this shoe!" Prince Billy said.

They each took turns, trying and yelling:
    "It fits! IT FITS! Ignore the swelling!"
"Does no one else live here?" asked Billy.
    They shook their heads: "No – don't be silly!"

Cinders knew what she should do.
    She picked up glass shoe number two,
then smashed it on a heavy rock
    and used the heel to pick the lock!

HOME

She ran upstairs and cried out, "Hey!
  I'll try that shoe on, if I may!"
And without Cinders forcing it,
  the shoe slipped on – the perfect fit!

The prince proposed: she was delighted!
(Eve and Val were not invited.)
And though their feet got rather wet,
the pair were wed in a COURGETTE!

What happens next?

Some of the pictures from the story have been mixed up! Can you retell the story and point to each picture in the correct order?

Rhyming words

Read the words in the middle of each group and point to the other words that rhyme with them.

call

ball

get

long

small

dance

green

mean

queen

seat

cool

tool

help

pool

white

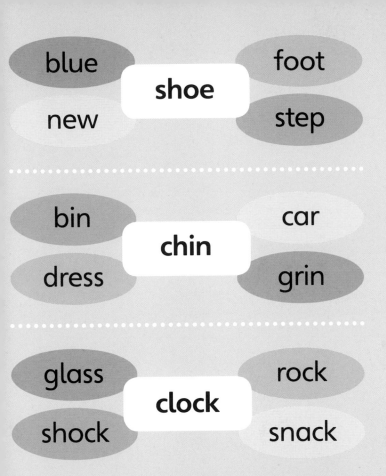

blue

foot

shoe

new

step

bin

car

chin

dress

grin

glass

rock

clock

shock

snack

Now choose a word and make up a rhyming chant!

The **new shoe** was bright **blue!**

Key words

These sentences use common words to describe the story. Read the sentences and then make up new sentences for the other words in the border.

Cinderella was locked **in** a cellar.

The prince **was** having a ball.

A courgette fairy appeared.

Cinderella **went** to the ball.

The prince **asked** for some food.

went · they

· are · but · made · day · an · can · we · him · up · ha

They ate some limousine **made** of courgette.

Cinderella left **one** glass shoe behind.

The prince **looked** for Cinderella.

Cinderella tried **on** the shoe.

Cinderella married **the** prince.

the · a · and · to · see · in · was · I · looked · he · you · of · she · on · for · when

· her · is · asked · one · at · then · have · so · be ·

Picture dictionary

Look carefully at the pictures and the words.
Now cover the words, one at a time.
Can you remember how to write them?

clock

fairy

girl

limousine

lock

prince

shoe

sister

soap